TIME TO PLAY SOCCER!

Adapted by Gloria Cruz
Ready-to-Read

Simon Spotlight
New York   Amsterdam/Antwerp   London   Toronto   Sydney/Melbourne   New Delhi
An imprint of Simon & Schuster Children's Publishing Division • 1230 Avenue of the Americas, New York, New York 10020 • This Simon Spotlight edition July 2025 • CoComelon™ & © 2025 Moonbug Entertainment. All Rights Reserved. • All rights reserved, including the right of reproduction in whole or in part in any form. SIMON SPOTLIGHT, READY-TO-READ, and colophon are registered trademarks of Simon & Schuster, LLC. • For information about special discounts for bulk purchases, please contact Simon & Schuster Special Sales at 1-866-506-1949 or business@simonandschuster.com. • Manufactured in the United States of America 0325 LAK • 10 9 8 7 6 5 4 3 2 1
ISBN 9781665970501 (hc) • ISBN 9781665970495 (pbk) • ISBN 9781665970518 (ebook)

Here is a list of all the words you will find in this book. Sound them out before you begin reading the story.

Names:

 Cody

 JJ

 Nina

Word families:

"-all"	→	all	ball	
"-ay"	→	away	day	play
"-ick"	→	kick	quick	

Sight words:

a	and	can	feet	good
have	her	his	in	is
like	make	of	she	stop
the	they	to	together	use
with				

Bonus words:

front	fun	goal	goalie
hands	score	soccer	stand
wants			

Ready to go? Happy reading!

Don't miss the questions about the story on the last page of this book.

JJ, Cody, and Nina like to play soccer!

JJ can kick the ball to Cody.

Cody wants to score a goal.

Cody can kick the ball with his feet.

Cody can make a goal!

Nina is the goalie.

She can stand in front of the goal.

Nina can use her hands.

Nina is quick!

Now that you have read the story, can you answer these questions?

1. Who kicks the ball and makes a goal?

2. Who stands in front of the goal and stops the ball?

3. In this story you read the words "away," "day," and "play." Those words rhyme. Can you think of other words that rhyme with "away," "day," and "play"?

**Great job!
You are a reading star!**

JJ, Cody, and Nina have fun all day!

Nina is a good goalie!

Nina can kick the ball away.

Nina can stop the ball!